TIME-TURNER

Behind-the-Scenes with
Hermione's Magical Artifact

By K.S. Dávila

San Rafael, California

INTRODUCTION

Have you ever wished you had more time in the day to do all the things you want to do? Or perhaps you've wished you could be in several places at once? Hermione Granger certainly feels that way as she enters her third year at Hogwarts School of Witchcraft and Wizardry, when she signs up for more classes than time will physically allow. Determined to attend them all, the bright young witch secures special permission from Professor McGonagall (the Deputy Headmistress of Hogwarts) and the Ministry of Magic to use a special device called a Time-Turner, which allows its user to turn time backward and relive the same hours over again.

But as one of Harry Potter's best friends, Hermione inevitably finds herself involved in a life-or-death rescue before long. And the power to turn back time just might come in handy when trying to save a life or two!

HERMIONE'S TIME-TURNER

Making its appearance in *Harry Potter and the Prisoner of Azkaban*, Hermione Granger's Time-Turner is made of a tiny hourglass set within a golden gyroscope. It is inscribed with the words, "Each turn of the hourglass sends the user back one hour." Throughout her third year, Hermione wears her Time-Turner on a chain around her neck, hidden beneath the collar of her shirt, so that she can secretly use it to attend multiple classes at the same time. Nobody notices she's been walking around the school in several places at once—not even her best friends Harry Potter and Ron Weasley! Harry only learns the truth when she pulls him back in time to rescue Sirius Black.

"Don't be silly, Ronald. How could anyone be in two classes at once?"
—Hermione Granger,
Harry Potter and the Prisoner of Azkaban

DESIGNING THE TIME-TURNER

Envisioning the Time-Turner wasn't easy. Concept artist Dermot Power sketched out numerous possible designs for the prop, placing the hourglass-shaped element within clocks, vials, and pendants. Later graphic artist Miraphora Mina expanded on these sketches in creating her own design.

When Miraphora was given the task of creating the Time-Turner prop, she knew she wanted the piece to be inconspicuous enough that Hermione could successfully hide it when necessary, but she also wanted to have an element that moved. The Time-Turner Miraphora designed is flat, but when Hermione uses it, "it comes alive," Miraphora says. "It becomes 3-D because it's really a ring within a ring that opens up to allow part of it to spin." Mina also needed to develop a way for Harry and Hermione to use the Time-Turner together. "The script described an action where Hermione extends the chain to circle her and Harry," Mina continues, "so it was created with a double catch that allowed the chain to widen to fit around them both."

The final touch to the piece of golden jewelry was the two mottos about time Mina had engraved upon it. The inscription on the outside ring reads, "I mark the hours every one, Nor have I yet outrun the sun," and on the inside ring, "My use a value, unto you, Are gauged by what you have to do."

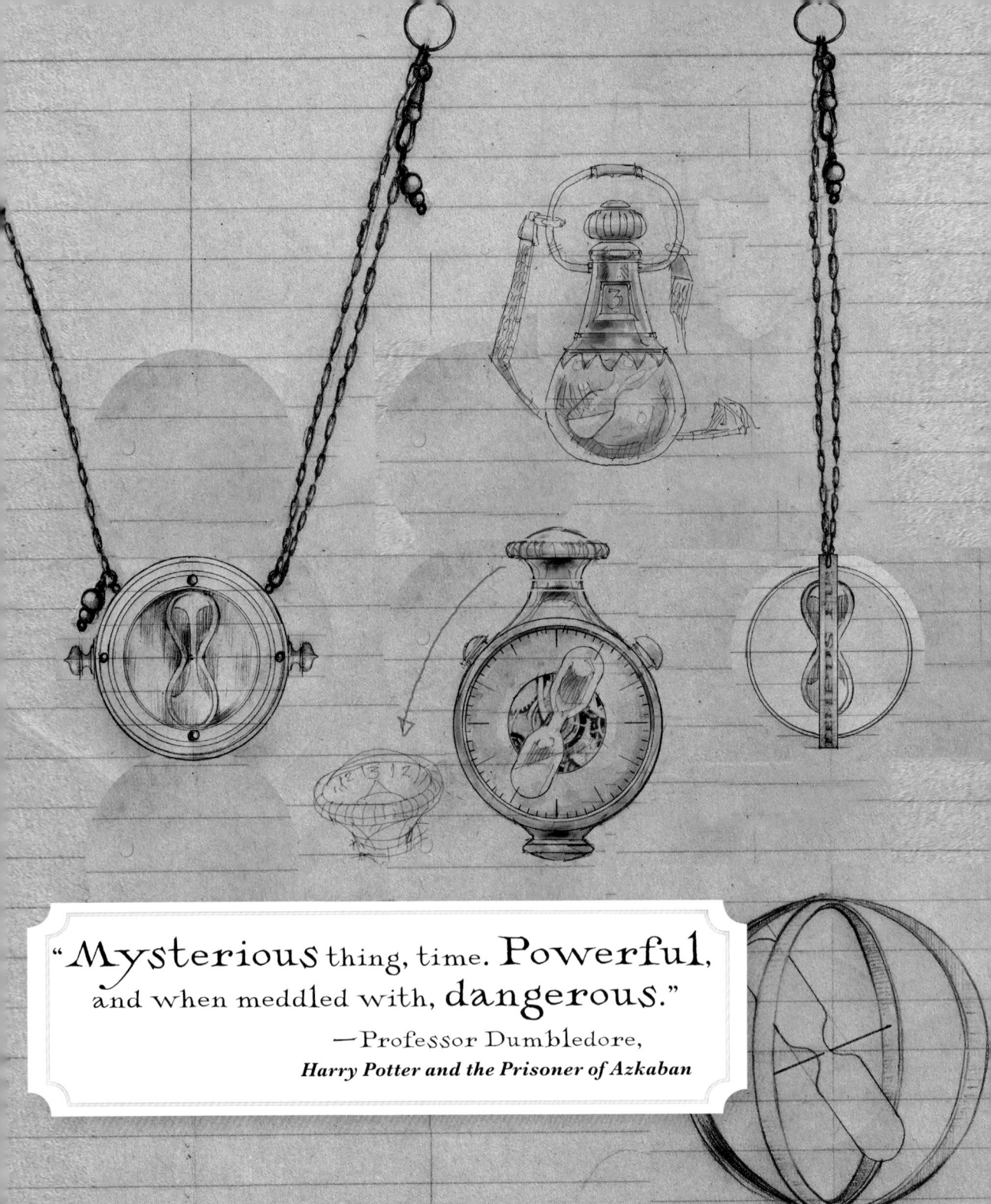

"Mysterious thing, time. Powerful, and when meddled with, dangerous."
—Professor Dumbledore,
Harry Potter and the Prisoner of Azkaban

THE TROUBLE WITH TIME TRAVEL

Is it possible to change the past? In *Harry Potter and the Prisoner of Azkaban*, Hermione uses her Time-Turner to transport Harry Potter and herself three hours back in time in order to save the life of Sirius Black. However, they must avoid crossing paths with their past selves as well as actually changing the past. "If you just go bursting in, you'll think you've gone mad," Hermione explains, warning Harry not to confuse his past self. "Awful things happen to wizards who've meddled with time. We can't be seen."

When they go back in time, Harry and Hermione learn that they are actually responsible for creating some of the incidents that they experienced before they turned back the clock. For example, while hiding from Buckbeak the Hippogriff's executioner in Hagrid's hut, Harry is hit in the back of the head by a mysterious stone, which alerts him that the executioner is approaching. After using the Time-Turner, Harry learns that time-traveling Hermione is the one who threw that stone to warn him of the danger. And at one point, when Harry and Hermione are cornered by the werewolf Remus Lupin, they are saved by a strange distant howl that distracts Lupin so they can get away. We later discover that time-traveling Hermione produced this sound in order to save them.

HAVE YOU SEEN THIS WIZARD?

In the beginning of *Harry Potter and the Prisoner of Azkaban*, Harry Potter learns that a dangerous murderer named Sirius Black has escaped from Azkaban, a magical maximum security prison for the most dangerous witches and wizards. And even worse, Harry's friends suspect that Sirius Black wishes to find Harry Potter and kill him.

The first time Harry sees the face of Sirius Black is on a wanted poster. "He had to look like he'd been in Azkaban," explains Amanda Knight, chief makeup designer. "His eyes, very deep set, haunted. Teeth, rotting. We designed these tattoos! His whole body was absolutely covered in tattoos all down his arms, and it's a very scary image when you first see that." His fearsome face is plastered everywhere—on the front of the *Daily Prophet*, in the Leaky Cauldron, and in the village of Hogsmeade.

As photographs in the wizarding world move, Sirius Black's mug shot shows him in motion, shouting and thrashing about like a wild man. This wanted poster provides an evocative introduction to an important character who otherwise wouldn't make his first appearance on-screen until more than halfway through the film. The magical moving wanted posters were achieved using miniature green-screen areas, which were then filled with the moving image of a screaming Sirius.

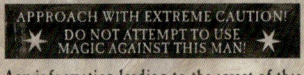

"Well, well, Sirius. Looking rather ragged aren't we? Finally the flesh reflects the madness within."

—Professor Lupin,
Harry Potter and the Prisoner of Azkaban

THE PRISONER OF AZKABAN

Throughout the first half of *Harry Potter and the Prisoner of Azkaban*, Sirius Black seems to be the villain. Harry believes that Sirius, who was his father's best friend, is the one who betrayed his parents to Lord Voldemort. However, in a twist, Harry discovers that Sirius Black is in fact a good man who has been framed. And he is about to be executed for crimes he didn't commit! Harry and Hermione must turn back the clock to save him.

Sirius Black goes from frightening to friendly. "So, we needed an actor who could play danger, and who could then embrace the tenderness and affection of this character," explains Alfonso Cuarón, director of *Harry Potter and the Prisoner of Azkaban*. "It was an immediate decision to go with Gary Oldman." Actor Gary Oldman sees his character, Sirius Black, as "a man very much haunted, living in the past and emotionally rooted in the old days. Harry is so like James [Harry's father], who was my friend—whom I adored—so I am living a friendship through him and wanting him to be like James."

BUCKBEAK THE HIPPOGRIFF

On their journey back in time, Harry and Hermione seek to save not just one life but two. On their way to rescue Sirius Black, they also save Buckbeak, a Hippogriff facing certain death.

A Hippogriff is a magical beast with the head, wings, and front legs of an eagle and the hindquarters of a horse. As Hagrid explains, they are known to be very proud creatures, and it is perhaps Buckbeak's pride that gets him into trouble. When Draco Malfoy disrespects the wild beast, Buckbeak scratches his arm. Although the injury is minor, Draco complains to his father, Lucius Malfoy, who uses his considerable influence to send an executioner to the school to put Buckbeak down. Fortunately, Harry and Hermione are able to rescue the creature just in time!

"You do not want to insult a Hippogriff. It may just be the last thing you ever do!"
—Rubeus Hagrid,
Harry Potter and the Prisoner of Azkaban

IT'S ALL IN THE DETAILS

To make Buckbeak look and feel real, and to give him his distinctive personality, the production team gave careful consideration to the tiniest of details. "One of the first things we did was go to the computer and ask, 'Okay, if it's a horse back-end with bird front legs, how does it move, how does it run, and how does it fly? Just how wide do the wings have to be to carry a creature the size of a horse?'" says Mark Radcliffe, an executive producer on the films. The creature department initially built a life-size Buckbeak using aquatronic machinery to ensure that his movements would be lifelike and fluid. He was covered in real bird feathers to give him a realistic look and feel. However, in the end, the director decided to rely on Tim Burke, Roger Guyett, and their visual effects team to create most of Buckbeak's movement digitally.

"A lot of attention went into how we could give the Hippogriff a sense of weight," says Alfonso Cuarón, director of *Prisoner of Azkaban*. "And once we got the main elements, it became more about animating the character and making it something that would be realistic. I mean, it's so realistic that if people watch carefully in the paddock scene, you will see he actually poos. Buckbeak poos! It's not a big deal; it's just a matter-of-fact thing that he does."

THE WHOMPING WILLOW

Hogwarts students tend to stay far, far away from the magical Whomping Willow, for fear of getting "whomped" by its big, angry branches. We first meet the perilous plant in *Harry Potter and the Chamber of Secrets,* when Ron and Harry crash Mr. Weasley's flying car into it and barely escape with their lives. But we learn in *Harry Potter and the Prisoner of Azkaban* that hidden at the base of the tree is a secret passageway into the Shrieking Shack in Hogsmeade.

While a full-size version of the tree was built on set for *Harry Potter and the Prisoner of Azkaban,* the filmmakers decided to add the branches in postproduction using computer-generated (CG) animation. In the scene where Harry and Hermione attempt to follow Sirius Black into the secret passage at the base of the tree, Daniel Radcliffe (Harry) and Emma Watson (Hermione) were harnessed to motion-controlled rigs and swung around according to choreographed movements. These shots were then enhanced with CG effects.

THE SHRIEKING SHACK

The Shrieking Shack is an old, creepy house on the edge of Hogsmeade Village. "It's meant to be the most haunted building in Britain," Hermione remarks. In *Harry Potter and the Prisoner of Azkaban*, a big black dog (who turns out to be Sirius Black) drags Ron Weasley from the Whomping Willow all the way into the rickety structure, as Harry and Hermione follow close behind. It's there that Harry, Ron, and Hermione learn the truth about Sirius Black—and Ron's pet rat, Scabbers.

When designing the Shrieking Shack, the production designer Stuart Craig wanted the place to have a distinctive character. "It needed to be creaking and moving, as if being continually buffeted by the wind," he explains. The filmmakers started by building a miniature model of the set to figure out how the building would move, and then they constructed the final set on a large hydraulic platform. "It had a massive steel frame that was pushed around by the hydraulics," says Craig. "Then we built the set to hang on to the frame." Due to the way the set was constructed, every piece of the structure was able to tilt and move, from the walls to the doors to the shutters. Unfortunately, this peculiar set created several potential issues for the filmmakers. "The creaking of the walls was so loud," says actor Daniel Radcliffe (Harry Potter), "sometimes we couldn't actually hear what the other was saying." Alfonso Cuarón recalls that, "Some people got motion sickness just because of the walls moving like that!"

MAKE IT YOUR OWN

One of the great things about IncrediBuilds™ models is that each one is completely customizable. The untreated, natural wood can be decorated with paints, pencils, pens, beads, sequins—the list goes on and on!

Before you start building and decorating your model, read through the included instruction sheet so you understand how all the pieces come together. Then choose a theme—do you want to create a replica or something completely different? The possibilities are endless! Here are some sample projects to get those creative juices flowing.

WHAT YOU NEED:

- Paints (gold, light blue or white, brown)
- Paintbrush
- Black pen

STEPS:

1. Paint the model, except for the hourglass, gold. Paint the edges of each ring carefully, letting them dry with the rings open (not flat) so they don't stick together.

2. Paint the sand of the hourglass light brown.

3. To represent the transparent glass, paint the rest of the hourglass light blue or white. Add a reflection detail by painting a curved line over the sand section.

4. Using a black pen add lettering to the outer and inner rings in four parts:
   I mark the hours, every one,
   Nor have I yet outrun the Sun.
   My use a value, unto you,
   Are gauged by what you have to do.

It's best to paint this model after it's fully assembled.

A Division of Insight Editions
PO Box 3088
San Rafael, CA 94912
www.insighteditions.com
www.incredibuilds.com

Find us on Facebook: www.facebook.com/InsightEditions
Follow us on Twitter: @insighteditions

 Copyright © 2018 Warner Bros. Entertainment Inc. HARRY POTTER characters, names and related indicia are © & ™ Warner Bros. Entertainment Inc. WB SHIELD: © & ™ WBEI. WIZARDING WORLD trademark and logo © & ™ Warner Bros. Entertainment Inc. Publishing Rights © JKR. (s18)

Published in 2018 by Insight Editions, LP, San Rafael, California. All rights reserved. No part of this book may be reproduced in any form without written permission from the publisher.

Library of Congress Cataloging-in-Publication Data available.

ISBN: 978-1-68298-204-4

Publisher: Raoul Goff
Associate Publisher: Vanessa Lopez
Art Director: Chrissy Kwasnik
Editor: Gregory Solano
Associate Managing Editor: Lauren LePera
Editorial Assistant: Hilary VandenBroek
Senior Production Editor: Rachel Anderson
Production Director: Lina s Palma
Model Designer: HeJian Zhu, TeamGreen

Insight Editions, in association with Roots of Peace, will plant two trees for each tree used in the manufacturing of this book. Roots of Peace is an internationally renowned humanitarian organization dedicated to eradicating land mines worldwide and converting war-torn lands into productive farms and wildlife habitats. Roots of Peace will plant two million fruit and nut trees in Afghanistan and provide farmers there with the skills and support necessary for sustainable land use.

Manufactured in China

10 9 8 7 6 5 4 3 2 1